MEET ALL THESE FRIENDS IN BUZZ BOOKS:

Thomas the Tank Engine
The Animals of Farthing Wood
Biker Mice From Mars
James Bond Junior
Fireman Sam
Joshua Jones
Rupert
Babar

First published in Great Britain by Buzz Books,
an imprint of Reed Children's Books
Michelin House, 81 Fulham Road, London SW3 6RB
and Auckland, Melbourne, Singapore and Toronto

Fireman Sam © copyright 1985 Prism Art & Design Limited
Text © copyright 1994 Reed International Books Limited
Illustrations © copyright 1994 Reed International Books Limited
Based on the animation series produced by Bumper Films
for S4C/Channel 4 Wales and Prism Art & Design Limited
Original idea by Dave Gingell and Dave Jones,
assisted by Mike Young. Characters created by Rob Lee.
All rights reserved.

ISBN 1 85591 385 2

Printed in Italy by Olivotto

THE GREAT
WATER TRAIL

Story by Rob Lee
Illustrations by The County Studio

There was a heatwave in Pontypandy.

"It's so hot!" said Station Officer Steele.

Just then, he received a telephone call from the town council. He listened for a minute, then hurried to the mess hall to see Firefighter Elvis Cridlington.

"There's an official drought," he told Elvis. "To save water, the supply for Pontypandy will be turned off for two hours beginning at midday. There's going to be a radio announcement to warn everyone."

Station Officer Steele bustled about. "We'd better check Jupiter's emergency supply just in case."

At Newtown Station, Firefighter Penny
Morris had also received a phone call.

"The water in Newtown won't be shut off
until late this afternoon," she thought. "I'll
drive over to Pontypandy now to see if I can
be of any help in the meantime."

Dilys and Norman were stacking the shelves in the shop. Dilys turned on the radio to hear the latest weather report.

"Phew," muttered Dilys, "I'm fed up with this heat. I can't wait for winter!"

Dilys was so busy complaining to Norman that they didn't hear the announcement on the radio.

Norman wanted to go out to play.

"I know, Mum," he said, "why don't you close the shop for the rest of the day?"

"Well, it is quiet," said Dilys. "You're absolutely right, Norman! We'll close at lunchtime, then I'll treat myself to a nice, cool bath!"

Meanwhile, Fireman Sam was enjoying a day off with the twins when he heard the radio announcement.

"I know!" he said brightly, "I'll make a machine that can find water."

The twins thought this was a great idea.

In his inventing shed, Fireman Sam attached some springs and some nuts and bolts to bits of metal. Then he fixed a small T.V. aerial to the front of the machine.

"Bingo!" he cried. "One automatic divining machine."

"Brilliant!" said Sarah. "But what's a divining machine?"

"It will help us to find water," said Sam. "Let's try it out."

Sam pressed a button and the automatic divining machine sprang to life. Fireman Sam and the twins followed, as it clanked merrily towards the countryside.

Sam and the twins followed the divining machine for what seemed like miles.

"Not a peep!" moaned James. "I don't think it works, Uncle Sam."

But as Fireman Sam bent down to inspect his invention, the lights on the divining machine began flashing and it sped off into a clump of bushes, beeping loudly.

Nearby, Trevor Evans had parked his bus in
a lay-by. He sat on the grass verge to enjoy
his lunch.

"Boyo, am I thirsty," he said, opening his
bottle of mineral water.

Suddenly, the divining machine burst
through the bushes, beeping frantically.

16

"Daro!" exclaimed Trevor, jumping up in alarm. "What is that?"

Sam appeared behind the machine. When he saw Trevor's bottle of water, he started to laugh.

"Well, now we know the divining machine works!" he chuckled.

Just after midday, Dilys put the CLOSED
sign on the shop door.

"You go out and play, my little treasure,"
she said to Norman. "I'm going to have
that bath."

Dilys turned the bath taps on, but nothing
came out.

"Oh no! The plumbing must be broken,"
she wailed. "And I'm so hot. I suppose I'll
have to make do with a cool drink at Bella's
café instead."

Dilys sighed heavily. Forgetting to turn
the taps off, she made her way across the
road to the café.

Norman had run off to look for Sarah and James. He found them walking on the path beside Pandy River with Fireman Sam and a very strange looking contraption.

"The automatic divining machine is supposed to find water," James explained. "But the river is dry."

"Why don't we try somewhere else?" suggested Sarah.

20

After a while, they found a drop of water in the pond and some water in the trough at Pandy Farm, but that was all.

"It's no use," said James.

Sam looked at his watch.

"It's after two o'clock. The water supply will be back on in Pontypandy now anyway."

Sam, the children and the automatic divining machine all trooped back to town. As they reached the High Street, the machine suddenly began beeping loudly. It raced towards Dilys Price's shop. They all raced after it.

"Great fires of London!" cried Sam. "The shop is flooded!"

"Oh no," said Norman. "The bath has overflowed. But where's Mum?"

"I'll look for her," said Sam, racing into the shop. "You phone the fire brigade, Norman. Quickly!"

In the bathroom, Sam sloshed through the water to turn off the bath taps.

"Dilys!" he called.

She was nowhere to be found.

Through the window of Bella's café, Dilys noticed Jupiter racing down the High Street.

"I wonder what's happening," she said to Bella.

She went out to the pavement to look. It was then that she noticed the water streaming out of the upstairs window.

Quickly, Station Officer Steele and Penny set up the pumping equipment, while Elvis ran into the shop with some buckets.

The suction hoses drained the water from the bathroom and carried it to Jupiter's water tank. Elvis and Sam bailed the extra water with their buckets.

At last, there were only a few small puddles left in the bathroom. Dilys frowned as she inspected the damage.

"Don't worry," said Fireman Sam. "The bathroom won't take long to dry out in this weather. And the water wasn't wasted. It's just topped up our emergency supply."

Later, everyone gathered outside Bella's café for a nice, cool drink.

"I'd better get back to Newtown," said Penny. "The water supply is due to be turned off there shortly."

Suddenly, Sam felt a drip on his head.

Then the rain poured down from the sky.

"Well, I think this means our drought is over," chuckled Fireman Sam.

Everyone laughed and enjoyed the rain, and the automatic divining machine spun round in circles, beeping madly!

FIREMAN SAM

STATION OFFICER
STEELE

TREVOR EVANS

ELVIS
CRIDLINGTON

PENNY MORRIS